The Spirit of

HIAWATHA

The Spirit of
HIAWATHA

Written
and illustrated by

DEMi

Ignatius

The Iroquois people of North America long believed that the Master of Life had told them to live peacefully with one another. Over time, the people drifted apart and broke into five different tribes who fought one another constantly.

In the late 1500s, an Iroquois named Hiawatha came up with a plan. To restore peace and to unify his people, he brought the Iroquois tribes together in a federation. They named it the League of Five Nations.

When French Jesuit priests arrived to convert the native peoples to Christianity in the 1600s, the Iroquois killed some of them. Yet more brave Black Robes (as they were called) arrived to take their place. In 1654, the Black Robes sought the leaders of the League of Five Nations and made peace with the Iroquois.

Such harmony would not have been possible without the visionary Hiawatha, who had prepared the way for the Gospel in North America.

Hiawatha, the great leader of the Iroquois, inspired many legends. It is said he was born around the year 1550 in the forests of New York.

Hiawatha grew strong and tall like a tree. At a young age, he learned to shoot wild game. During the freezing winters, he knew where to find berries hidden beneath the snow and potatoes buried in the ground.

When Hiawatha was older, he helped build the longhouses of his people. For the walls, the men cut long timbers and lashed them together. They laid elm bark shingles over roofs made of saplings.

To train for war, the men played lacrosse, a game where two teams fought fiercely with netted sticks for a deerskin ball.

roquois men also went on very dangerous hunts. They tracked bears, wolves, and wild boar. They chose the bravest, swiftest, and strongest among them to be their leaders.

Hiawatha knew that long ago the Iroquois had been one people. But in his day, they were always fighting. Sometimes they fought over hunting grounds. Other times they fought for their honor. More and more, it seemed to Hiawatha, they fought for no good reason at all.

When Hiawatha reached full manhood, he was strong and handsome. He married a beautiful woman, who bore seven lovely daughters. Hiawatha was also wise and well-spoken, and his people made him a chief. He began urging them to stop fighting needless wars, and they listened to him.

But power had twisted the mind of one chief, Tadodaho. Tadodaho was dishonest and cruel, and the people feared him. Snakes lived in his long, tangled hair. A jealous man, Tadodaho killed Hiawatha's wife and daughters.

Filled with grief and anger, Hiawatha fled deep into the forest. He vowed never to live among men again. He made himself a hut of tree boughs in a lonely place where no one could find him.

But someone did find him—the great Deganawidah. Whether Deganawidah was man or spirit, Hiawatha could not tell, but he took away Hiawatha's sorrow and desire for revenge. Then Deganawidah gave him a vision for making peace among the five tribes.

Deganawidah described a giant spruce tree whose upper branches broke through the sky into the everlasting light. It was the Great Tree of Peace, and its roots were the five tribes.

At the top of the tree an eagle perched, watching constantly in all directions for enemies who would disturb the peace.

eganawidah said to Hiawatha: "Before this vision can come true, you must love your enemies and do good to those who harm you." Then he told Hiawatha to return to his tribe and forgive Tadodaho.

With the greatest courage, Hiawatha went. He told Tadodaho that he forgave him. Then he combed the snakes from his hair, and the man's evil thoughts left him. (The name Hiawatha means "he-who-combs.")

adodaho was his true self again, and the people were amazed. Deganawidah came to their tribe and taught everyone the way of forgiveness.

Deganawidah said that for the Great Tree of Peace to become a reality, he needed to bring the message of forgiveness to the other four tribes.

He had a bad stammer, so he asked Hiawatha to go with him, to speak on his behalf. Thus, he and Hiawatha went to the other tribes together.

With his gift of speech, Hiawatha helped Deganawidah. They softened hearts, smoothed over past hatreds, and restored harmony wherever they went. Soon all the leaders of the five tribes were ready to meet in a council.

Around the council fire, the Mohawk, Onondaga, Oneida, Cayugaa, and Seneca became one Iroquois family again. They called themselves the League of Five Nations.

eganawidah knew that even with the federation, there would still be war. There were tribes outside the Iroquois nations, and they were still enemies. Thus, he made a way for making peace with them too.

"I plant the Tree of Great Peace among you," Deganawidah said. "But if a man of any nation outside the Five Nations shall desire to obey the laws of the Great Peace, he shall be welcome to take shelter under the Tree."

Deganawidah asked the chiefs of the five tribes to find the tallest pine tree in the forest. He told them to remove the tree without harming it, by digging deeply around its roots.

"Cast your weapons into the hole that held the roots of this great tree," he said. "Bury them from sight forever by replanting the tree on top of them."

And so, to this day, when we let go of a grudge we speak of "burying the hatchet."

Deganawidah's work was finished. "Now I go where none can follow me," he said. He walked to the shore of the lake and entered a white canoe made of stone. Then he paddled westward and disappeared into the setting sun while all the Iroquois wept.

Hiawatha still had much to do. With beads made of clam shells, he sewed symbols onto five pieces of leather. These were the first wampum belts, and they signified the constitution of the League of Five Nations.

Hiawatha gave each tribe a belt. It would help the Iroquois remember the agreements they had made to live in peace with one another.

The League of Five Nations was still in place when Europeans began to arrive in North America. Its constitution was admired by Thomas Jefferson and Benjamin Franklin, who studied it while founding the United States.

The constitutions of the United States and the League of Five Nations share much in common. Each includes:

    1. the joining together of separate states or nations into one country or federation;

    2. representative government, where each state or nation sends representatives to the central government;

    3. one vote for each representative;

    4. separation of powers and checks and balances through three branches of government;

    5. a highest court to interpret the people's laws.

After Hiawatha finished the task of unifying his people, his time on earth was at an end. Like his master before him, he went to the lakeshore and entered a snow-white canoe. He bade farewell and paddled away, vanishing into the clear white light.

Although Hiawatha was no longer present with his people, his spirit continued to inspire peace among the members of the League of Five Nations.

The League still fought wars with tribes outside the alliance. When French Jesuit priests and brothers arrived in New York to spread the Good News about Jesus, they set up missions among the Huron, who were enemies of the Iroquois. From 1642 to 1649, Iroquois captured and killed eight Jesuit missionaries.

Other Jesuits bravely replaced these North American Martyrs. They sought the leaders of the League of Five Nations to offer their forgiveness. In the spirit of Hiawatha, the chiefs accepted the peace of Christ and allowed the Gospel to be preached among their people.

Among those who accepted the Good News was the Mohawk maiden Kateri Tekakwitha. Born in 1656, she followed Christ with all her heart, and she became the first Native American to be named a saint.

In 1722, the Tuscarora joined the League, which was then renamed the Six Nations.

The Six Nations still exists today, with about 125,000 enrolled members living in Canada and the United States.

The alliance is held together by a shared history and culture, thanks to the visionary leadership of Hiawatha hundreds of years ago.

Editors: Isabelle Galmiche, Vivian Dudro
Proofreader: Kathleen Hollenbeck
Layout Designer: Gauthier Delauné
Production: Thierry Dubus, Sabine Marioni

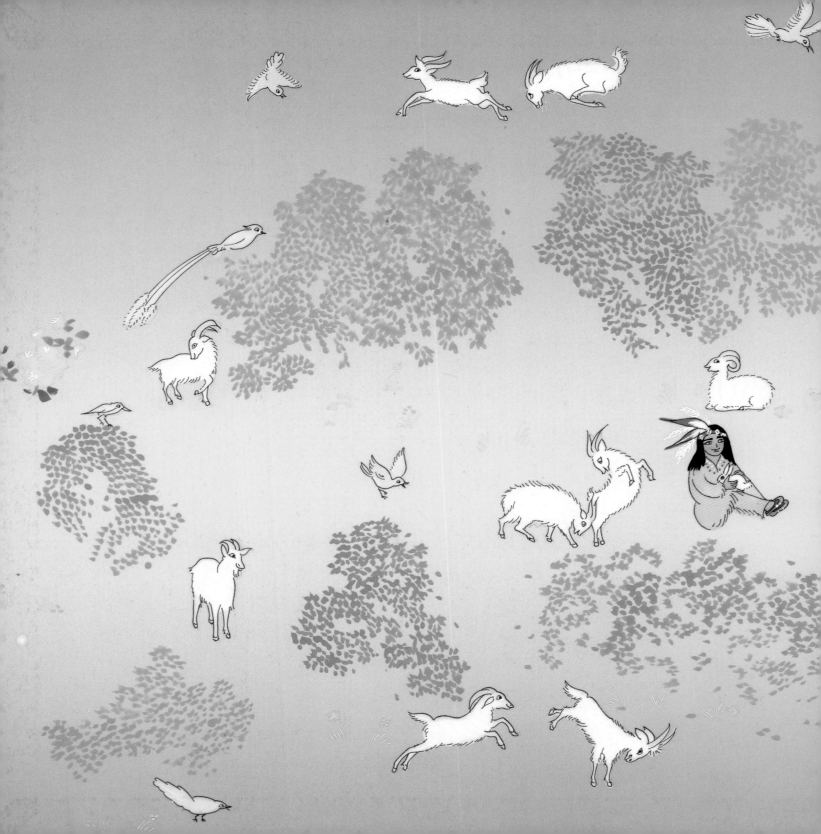